NORTHANGER ABBEY

JANE AUSTEN

REAL READS

www.realreads.co.uk

Retold by Gill Tavner
Illustrated by Ann Kronheimer

Published by Real Reads Ltd
Stroud, Gloucestershire, UK
www.realreads.co.uk

Text copyright © Gill Tavner 2008
Illustrations copyright © Ann Kronheimer 2008
The right of Gill Tavner to be identified as author of this book
has been asserted by her in accordance with the
Copyright, Design and Patents Act 1988

First published in 2008

ISBN 978-1-906230-08-1

Printed in China by Imago Ltd
Designed by Lucy Guenot
Typeset by Bookcraft Ltd, Stroud, Gloucestershire

CONTENTS

THE CHARACTERS

Catherine Morland

Catherine is an unlikely heroine. Is she strong enough for the challenges that lie ahead? Will she live happily ever after?

James Morland

James is Catherine's brother. Will his friendship with John Thorpe lead him and Catherine to happiness or heartbreak?

Isabella Thorpe

At twenty-one years old, Isabella is beautiful, fashionable and more experienced than Catherine. Is she a true friend? Can Catherine and James trust her?

John Thorpe

Isabella's brother and James's friend.
Will he be the hero of Catherine's
story, or the villain?

Henry Tilney

Henry is an intelligent, pleasant
clergyman. Can such a man be a hero?
Why is he afraid of his father? What
does he think of Catherine?

Eleanor Tilney

Henry's younger sister is shy and
gentle. How did her mother die?
Why is she afraid of her father?

General Tilney

Henry and Eleanor's father is both
charming and frightening. Why are
his children afraid of him? What
dreadful secrets is he hiding in
Northanger Abbey?

NORTHANGER ABBEY

To be a true heroine, a girl must be beautiful and brave. She needs a wicked stepmother, like poor Cinderella, or a cruel father who locks her in a dark tower, or at least something that requires her to show her true mettle.

Our heroine, however, is different; perhaps even unique. Catherine Morland's appearance, like her name, was not likely to catch anybody's attention. Lively and playful as a child, Catherine did not pass lonely days gazing longingly through dusty windows, awaiting her handsome prince. Instead, she spent her childhood rolling down the green slope outside her house and playing happily with her nine brothers and sisters. Most surprisingly of all, Catherine's parents, in spite of having so many children to care for, were not only still living, but were happy and healthy. Although they were not very rich, neither were they very poor, and within the means available to them they loved all their children equally. However great the temptation must sometimes have been, they had never locked a child in a tower or sold a single baby to a passing witch.

Having survived unscathed to the age of seventeen, Catherine was ready to seek adventure. Her only experience of the world consisted of the small community around her parents' home and the worlds she imagined as she sat enthralled by her books. No hero had ever galloped up to her house or leapt from the pages of her book. Even Catherine's parents agreed that the time had come for their daughter to experience new places and new faces.

When their neighbour, Mrs Allen, offered to take Catherine to the fashionable city of Bath for a few weeks, everybody was delighted. As Catherine sat in the carriage ready to depart, her mother gave her advice which would be valuable for any heroine setting out on her first adventure: 'Make sure you keep account of the money you spend.' Catherine nodded, kissed her parents, and turned her eyes towards Bath.

Bath's Pump Rooms were the place to see and be seen. Understanding that a heroine ought to make a strong first impression, Mrs Allen was very particular about the gown Catherine should wear for her first appearance. Therefore, on her first full day in Bath, the finely-dressed Catherine stepped, wide-eyed, into the bustling Lower Rooms. Astonishingly, silence did not fall upon the crowd, and no gentleman gazed in rapturous wonder. One man, yawning, did comment to his friend that a girl who was 'almost pretty' had just entered the room. Almost unnoticed and almost pretty, our heroine took her first tentative steps into society.

Poor Catherine was overwhelmed by the largest crowd of people she had ever seen,

and heard with alarm that Mrs Allen did not
know anybody in the room. 'How disagreeable
this is,' complained Mrs Allen. 'I do wish we
had a large acquaintance in Bath.' Catherine
wished they had just one acquaintance in Bath.
It felt very awkward to have nobody to sit with.

'Catherine,' said Mrs Allen, suddenly,
'there are two gentlemen walking towards us.
Straighten your gown and flatten your hair,
dear. Oh, one of them seems quite familiar.
Isn't that ... '

'James!' gasped Catherine, her face showing joyful surprise as she watched her older brother advancing towards them. What was he doing in Bath? After an affectionate reunion, James introduced Catherine to his friend, a fellow student at Oxford. John Thorpe, a stout young man with a plain face and easy manners, gave a low bow. 'Miss Morland, we heard that you were in town, and have hurried from Oxford in the hope of seeing you. My horses have travelled

at no less than ten miles an hour. Isn't that so, Morland? It's a dashed good thing that we didn't bring your brother's carriage; he drives too slowly and his horses are so lumbering.' Catherine smiled politely. John Thorpe leaned towards her and whispered in her ear, 'I am monstrously pleased to meet you. Our real intention was to visit my sister, the ugly girl over there. Morland is rather fond of her.'

John Thorpe guided Catherine and Mrs Allen across the room to meet his mother and his sister. 'Mother, this is Morland's sister, Miss Catherine Morland. Isn't she the most charming girl in the world?' Turning to his sister, he directed, 'You and she should be friends, Isabella.'

Far from being ugly, Isabella Thorpe was tall, beautiful and fashionable. Breaking away from her brief conversation with James, she graciously invited Catherine to take a turn with her about the room. 'I have just told

Mr Hunt over there that I will not dance with him,' Isabella confided to her surprised new friend. 'He is excessively disappointed.' She directed Catherine's gaze towards a gentleman who, it seemed to Catherine, looked rather happy as he led a young lady onto the dance floor. However, as Isabella was four years older than Catherine, Catherine assumed that she had the advantage of greater experience in such matters.

'You will be a great favourite with the men,' Isabella said, smiling down at her. 'By the way, do you prefer dark or fair men?'

'I have never really thought about it,' replied Catherine.

'Oh, your pretended innocence is charming, but I understand you entirely. You do not wish to give me a clue about somebody who has already captured your heart. Your secret is safe with me. I would do anything for a friend.' She paused, before whispering into Catherine's ear, 'How do you like my brother John?'

'I like him very much,' answered Catherine, hoping that her face did not reveal the truth that she did not like him at all.

Isabella smiled.

'Do you read books?' asked Catherine, eager to move to a new subject.

'Oh yes, I have just finished reading *The Mysteries of Udolpho*,' replied Isabella.

Catherine was delighted. 'I am reading

Udolpho at the moment. I have just got to the black veil.'

'Aren't you wild to know what is behind it?'

'Is it something frightening? Is it a skeleton?'

'Oh, I would not tell you for the world.'

'I love *Udolpho*,' enthused Catherine, 'it is such a frightening book.'

'When you finish, you must read *The Haunted Abbey*. Will you be here tomorrow? I shall bring it with me.'

Returning to the corner of the room in which Mrs Allen was now enjoying an animated conversation with Mrs Thorpe, Catherine and Isabella were joined again by their brothers. In spite of her protestations that she could not leave Catherine alone, Isabella allowed James to lead her into the dance.

'I suppose you and I are to stand up and jig it together too,' said the gallant John Thorpe. For the next fifteen minutes, Catherine found

herself being galloped around the dance floor. When John requested a second dance, she firmly replied, 'I am tired and do not mean to dance any more.'

That evening, Catherine went eagerly to bed. She looked forward to meeting her new friend again tomorrow, but sincerely hoped that John Thorpe was not destined to be the hero of her story. Tired as she was, she allowed herself the luxury of reading *Udolpho* by candlelight. She eventually fell asleep thoroughly, thrillingly frightened.

The following morning passed slowly. When the time arrived to return to the Lower Rooms, Catherine quickly realised that Isabella, who had boasted that she would do anything for a friend, had not kept her appointment. Noticing Catherine's disappointed face, the skilful Master of Ceremonies introduced her to a gentleman who had also just arrived. Could this be our hero?

Suitably tall for a hero, Henry Tilney was a few years older than Catherine and very close to being handsome. After an enjoyable dance at a sensible speed, Catherine and Henry sat down together to take tea.

'Well Miss Morland,' Henry smiled, 'I know what you will write in your journal tonight.

You will say that you chose your blue gown in which you believe you looked beautiful, but that you danced with a strange man who continued to harass you all afternoon.'

'Sir, I shall write no such thing,' replied Catherine, unsure whether to laugh.

'Good. I should greatly prefer you to write that you danced with a charming man who is a conversational genius.'

'But sir, I do not keep a journal.'

'No journal! That is not possible! Where else is a lady to record her trivial thoughts and imperfect grammar?'

A pretty young lady, with the same intelligent eyes as Henry, appeared at his side. 'Please ignore my brother's teasing,' she smiled shyly at Catherine. 'He has greater respect for our fair sex than would appear at present.'

Henry rose from his chair. 'Eleanor, allow me to introduce the charming Miss Morland whose gown, I am sure you will agree, is beautiful.' Eleanor and Catherine exchanged warm smiles. 'However,' continued Henry, looking concerned, 'I do not believe it will wash well. I am afraid it will fray terribly.' With this unheroic observation, Henry bowed gallantly. 'Ladies, if you will excuse me, I must now leave you to discuss me between yourselves.'

Eleanor and Catherine were left with a topic of considerable interest to the latter. She learned that Henry Tilney was a caring brother, who, although from a wealthy family, held the rather unheroic position in society of a clergyman. Occasionally venturing on other polite topics of conversation, they found enough of mutual interest to secure the beginning of a friendship. However, the frequency with which Catherine directed the conversation back to Henry led Eleanor to suspect that her new friend had made a terrible error for the heroine of a story. She was developing an interest in a gentleman without first ensuring that he was in love with her.

By the end of the afternoon, Catherine was delighted to have been engaged by Eleanor to join her and Henry for a country walk the following day. 'We shall call at twelve o'clock, unless it rains,' were Eleanor's parting words. Catherine was sure that it would not.

At noon the following day, it was raining. 'It will clear,' said Catherine, looking anxiously from her window. By twelve thirty, the rain had stopped. As Catherine looked hopefully down the street, instead of the Tilneys, she saw two open carriages clatter to a halt outside her door. John Thorpe jumped out of the first one and called up to Catherine's window. 'Make haste, make haste,' he urged her, 'we are going to Bristol and to Blaize Castle.'

Although greatly attracted by the idea of a castle, Catherine said firmly, 'I am already engaged for the afternoon. Mr and Miss Tilney said they would call at twelve, but it was raining. As it has now stopped, I expect that they will be here any minute.'

'The Tilneys? I know them,' laughed Thorpe. 'I have just seen them walking in the other direction. You are safe from them today and are free to come with us.'

Isabella and James joined in Thorpe's persuasion from the other carriage. Disappointed that her new friends had so easily forgone their appointment, Catherine reluctantly agreed to join the others, and within five minutes they were off.

They had only reached the end of Pulteney
Street when Catherine saw Henry and Eleanor
Tilney walking towards her house. They stopped
and looked in surprise as the carriage drove past.
'Oh, stop Mr Thorpe, pray stop!' called Catherine.
'I cannot go on, I must talk to Miss Tilney.'

John Thorpe laughed and drove his horses
forward.

'How could you tell me that you had seen them walking away?' asked Catherine angrily. She watched Henry and Eleanor, still staring after her, become smaller and smaller as the carriage moved further away. 'They will think me so rude. I really must talk to them. You must stop.'

John Thorpe did not stop. The rest of the day was far from agreeable. Thorpe saw no fault in his behaviour, and boasted all day about his horses. In spite of these animals' reputation for speed, the party did not reach Blaize Castle before it was time to turn back to Bath. Catherine found it difficult to be civil as she stepped from the carriage, released at last.

Early the next morning, Catherine hurried to call on Henry and Eleanor. They were both absent. She had to endure her agony until that evening, when she saw Henry at the theatre. During the interval, she was able to explain fully. He understood and accepted her apology. Catherine, feeling that she was the happiest girl in Bath, listened with sparkling eyes and a fluttering heart to everything Henry said. So clearly finding him irresistible, she gradually became so herself.

'Is not that Thorpe, over there, talking to my father?' asked Henry, pointing across the

theatre to where John Thorpe was indeed deep in conversation with a very distinguished-looking gentleman.

Before Catherine could reply, the bell rang for the start of the second act and Henry returned to his seat.

At the end of the performance, John Thorpe rushed to Catherine's side. 'I have just been talking to General Tilney,' he reported with some pride. 'He thinks you are the finest girl in Bath, and I agree.'

With no engagements for the next few days, Catherine was able to finish *Udolpho*. She greatly looked forward to discussing the ending with Isabella. When they did eventually meet, however, Isabella had other things to talk about.

'Oh, I have been unable to hide anything from your clever eyes,' exclaimed Isabella.

Catherine looked at her in wondering ignorance.

'Don't pretend you haven't seen that I am in love with your charming brother.'

'In love with James!' gasped Catherine, truly astonished.

'More than in love. We are engaged to be married. James has ridden home today to secure your parents' consent.'

'Oh, dearest Isabella, we are to be sisters,' cried Catherine joyfully.

John Thorpe entered the room, looking fidgety and nervous. 'Jolly good thing, this marrying. Don't you agree?'

Catherine agreed.

'I'm glad you agree with marriage,' he continued, relaxing slightly. 'Don't they say that one marriage leads to another?'

'I have not heard it,' replied Catherine.

When John had left, Isabella smiled. 'My brother is quite in love with you and believes that you love him. He means to ask you to marry him.'

Poor Catherine was truly surprised. 'Oh no, Isabella!' she exclaimed. 'Please stop him. Please apologise for me if I have misled him. I could not accept.'

'Very well,' replied her friend, who clearly had something more important on her mind. Isabella then looked at Catherine with a grave face. 'How much money do you think your parents will give James upon our marriage?'

'I am sure they will give him as much as they can afford,' replied Catherine, offended. Surely this should not be a consideration for somebody in love?

Isabella smiled. 'Of course, I have no interest in money. Where love is true, even poverty is wealth.'

Catherine pushed aside her unease, and once again enjoyed the prospect of having Isabella as a sister.

The following week, still wondering at Isabella's news, Catherine received another surprise. Eleanor Tilney approached her in the Lower Rooms. 'Catherine, we are all leaving Bath in a fortnight.' Catherine's face fell. 'Perhaps you would be so good … ' continued Eleanor shyly, 'it would make me very happy if … my father has asked if you would honour us with a visit to our home, Northanger Abbey.'

Such an invitation from the distinguished General Tilney was an unexpected honour.

'Northanger Abbey!' repeated Catherine. Her imagination immediately saw a decaying building with long dark passages and terrible secrets hidden behind black veils. As her passion for old buildings was second only to her growing passion for Henry Tilney, she readily accepted the invitation. All that was needed was her parents' consent. This was duly sent for, and given, and Catherine prepared for her new adventure.

When the day of departure finally arrived, General Tilney suggested that, as the weather was so fine, Catherine might like to travel in the open curricle with Henry. Catherine was as happy a being as ever existed.

Noticing the parcel of books on the seat next to his passenger, Henry commented, 'I see that you are a keen reader.'

Aware that many people disliked novels, Catherine blushed. 'I am sure that you do not read, sir.'

'Of course I read,' smiled Henry. 'The person who does not enjoy a good novel must be intolerably stupid.' Catherine smiled as he continued, 'Who can fail to enjoy a book in which the greatest powers of the mind and the most thorough knowledge of human nature are displayed in carefully chosen language? Who can fail to enjoy the lively wit and humour?'

'Have you read *Udolpho* or *The Haunted Abbey*?' asked Catherine.

'I have, although they are not quite the books I had in mind.'

'Is Northanger Abbey haunted?'

Henry's eyes twinkled with mischief. 'Do you

have a strong heart and nerves, Miss Morland? Will you be able to cope with your first night at Northanger?'

'Oh, I am sure I will not be scared.'

'You must be brave when the crooked old housekeeper takes you to your gloomy room at the abandoned end of the abbey.'

'I will, I will.'

'When you see that there is a heavy, locked chest in the darkest corner of your room, will you have the courage to sleep?'

Catherine's smile was fading. 'I am sure this will not happen to me,' she said quietly, 'will it?'

'How will you feel when the housekeeper tells you about the tragic death that occurred in your room, and confides in you that she hears eerie noises on stormy nights?'

'Oh, please stop!'

Too much amused by Catherine's reactions to continue, Henry concentrated on guiding his gentle horses steadily towards Northanger Abbey.

The approach to Northanger Abbey was disappointingly modern. Even though the gathering grey clouds limited the sun's friendly rays, Catherine could clearly see that no part of the building was derelict or neglected.

The cheerful housekeeper led Catherine up a broad oak staircase to her room. The room was light and bright, with colourful wallpaper and a soft carpet. Catherine felt rather silly for having expected anything different. A large ebony cabinet in the corner of the room briefly sent a thrill through her body, before she remembered that General Tilney had told them not to be late for dinner. Catherine hurriedly changed, and found her way to the large and lofty hall where she was to meet her hosts.

Over dinner, Henry and Eleanor were not in their usual good spirits. Having expected to see them at their best, in the easy comfort of their own family, Catherine was disappointed to find them withdrawn and sullen.

Their father, on the other hand, was exceedingly civil towards her. It seemed that his only care was to entertain her and make her happy. His conversation was so full of gratitude and compliments that she felt quite awkward. Unable to relax in his presence, Catherine wondered whether his children were, like her, awed and somewhat crushed by his powerful personality. Could they be afraid of him?

Catherine returned to her room that evening relieved to be free from the General's civility. The night had grown stormy, and the two candles in her room cast strange shadows on the unfamiliar walls. As Catherine prepared for bed, she glanced repeatedly at the ebony cabinet. 'What is in it?' she wondered. 'Why is it pushed back into that dark corner?'

Catherine's curiosity must be satisfied before she could sleep. Taking a candle, she approached the cabinet with a beating heart. In the flickering light, she saw a key in its door.

She paused for a moment in breathless wonder.
Though the key turned, the door would not
open. It was not until Catherine learnt to turn
it once to the left and twice to the right that it
yielded to her fingers. A secret lock must hide a
terrible secret. Eyes straining, Catherine stared
at something in the drawer. It was a manuscript.
Her trembling hand reached towards it.

Suddenly, a violent wind blew out both
candles. Our brave heroine was plunged into
impenetrable darkness.

With a sharp shriek, Catherine dropped the paper. In a cold sweat, she groped her way to bed. Trembling underneath the covers, Catherine listened to the wind's haunting murmurs and moans for several hours before she fell asleep.

A cheerful ray of morning sun shone straight onto the abandoned manuscript where it lay on the floor. Catherine leapt out of bed, eagerly picked it up, and returned to bed to read it.

She slowly turned over the first page. She could not believe her eyes. Catherine was holding in her hands a list of clothes – a laundry bill!

'Oh, I have been so silly!' she gasped. Grateful that nobody knew of her adventure, she quickly returned the list to its drawer. The lock was now easy to open, and she realised that it was she herself who had locked it. 'From now on I shall be guided by common sense,' Catherine vowed.

After breakfast, Henry had to leave on parish business, and General Tilney offered to show Catherine around the abbey's grounds. Eleanor joined them. Following his purposeful stride, Catherine was filled with wonder as the vast grounds opened up before her. The General looked pleased.

'If I love anything, it is a good garden,' he said proudly, 'and I do believe that these grounds are the best in England.' Catherine said that she had never seen anything to rival them. 'I'm sure your father's grounds are similar.' he ventured. Catherine had to admit that the garden of her small cottage was of a quite different scale. 'You are too modest,' smiled General Tilney.

'Father, let's go this way,' suggested Eleanor.

'Why do you always choose that cold, damp path?' asked her father, a little irritably.

Timidly, Eleanor answered, 'It is my favourite walk.'

'Wander as you please,' said General Tilney. Catherine thought he looked rather angry as he turned away from Eleanor's chosen path and headed back towards the abbey.

The path was delightfully narrow, winding and overgrown. 'This was my mother's favourite walk,' Eleanor told Catherine. 'I used to walk here with her before she died.' She fell silent.

Eleanor's silence allowed Catherine to wonder. Why did General Tilney not like to go there? Surely his wife's favourite walk should be a favourite of the grieving husband. If he did not love his wife's walk, had he ever loved her? There was undoubtedly something harsh in the General's face. He must have been a cruel husband. Mrs Tilney must have suffered terribly in her marriage.

'Was your mother beautiful?'

'Very.'

'I presume that a portrait of her hangs in your father's room.'

'No, it hangs in mine. I will show you later.'

Catherine began to feel a terrified dislike towards General Tilney. Why could he not bear his wife's portrait in his room? How had she died?

That same afternoon, when General Tilney offered to show Catherine around the abbey itself, she felt a thrill of anticipation. With a dignified stride, the General led Catherine and Eleanor around the modern part of the abbey. It was furnished with great taste and at what must have been great expense. The General proudly listed the many distinguished visitors he had received at the abbey, and

added smilingly that he hoped one day to have reason to be honoured by a visit from her family. Astonished by such a hint at future relations, Catherine was silent.

They continued their tour through vast rooms and busy kitchens until they reached a heavy door at the end of a long gallery. Eleanor was about to open the door when her father said sharply, 'Stop, Eleanor. Surely Miss Morland has seen enough.'

Eleanor quickly allowed the door to close. Later, when they were alone, Eleanor whispered, 'I was about to take you into the gallery leading to my mother's room, the room in which she died nine years ago.'

'Were you with her when she died?' asked Catherine.

'No,' sighed Eleanor, 'I was away. It was a short and sudden illness.'

Catherine's blood ran cold with horrid thoughts. Was it possible ... ? Could Henry's father ... ? She determined to explore for herself the forbidden corridor and the room of death. Perhaps Mrs Tilney was not dead, but was kept a prisoner by her cruel husband. His behaviour certainly suggested a mind and spirit ill at ease.

Two hours before sunset, when General Tilney and his daughter were engaged downstairs, and Henry was still absent, Catherine seized her opportunity. She slid silently along the gallery. Breathlessly, she gently pushed the heavy door. It yielded easily.

Inside, Catherine found the room exactly as Mrs Tilney had left it nine years ago. Although it was no longer used, it was kept fresh and clean. There were no signs of neglect, no signs of a desperate struggle, and certainly no signs of an imprisoned wife. Suddenly, Catherine felt sick with shame. Hadn't she vowed to be guided by common sense?

Desperate to return to her room, Catherine was suddenly startled by the sound of heavy footsteps. What should she do? What if it was the General himself? Trembling, she hurried through the door, straight into the astonished Henry Tilney.

'Mr Tilney!' she gasped. 'Good god! Why are you here?'

'Why am I here?' repeated Henry in equal astonishment. 'Why, it is the shortest route from the stables to my room. But you, Miss Morland, why are you here? This is surely the longest route to your room.'

Catherine looked down at her feet. 'I have been to see your mother's room,' she confessed, 'because your father did not show me.' She paused for a moment and then could no longer resist the temptation to ask, 'How did your mother die?'

Studying the mixture of shame and curiosity visible on Catherine's face, Henry guessed her thoughts. 'The world never saw a better woman than my mother,' he told Catherine, sitting her down on his mother's bed. 'My father was not the easiest husband, but he sincerely valued her. He and I stayed by her bedside throughout her final illness. He called upon numerous surgeons but none could save her.'

'But ... '

'Miss Morland, consider the dreadful nature of your suspicions! I was with her when she died.'

'Oh!' Covering her face with shame, Catherine ran to her room. Hating herself and the silly books that had filled her head with such nonsense, she lay on her bed weeping bitter tears. Surely all was now lost with Henry? At that moment, with all hope gone, our heroine realised that she had lost her heart to him.

At breakfast the following morning, Henry understood that the poor, mortified Catherine needed comfort. He treated her with more gentleness and kindness than ever before. Catherine was grateful for such attention. She cheered up still further when Eleanor handed her an envelope addressed to her in James' handwriting. However, Henry and Eleanor were most concerned to see the blood drain from her face as she read the first sentence.

'Oh no, poor James!' she exclaimed. Tears filled her eyes and ran down her cheeks. 'All is at an end between James and Isabella,' she explained before reading on through her sobs. It seemed that both she and James had entirely misjudged Isabella's friendship. When she had discovered that the Morlands were not as wealthy as she had thought, Isabella had turned her charms upon a wealthier gentleman. James was heartbroken. 'Thank god I have discovered her character before it was too late!' he concluded.

Watching Catherine's compassionate tears falling, Henry softly and warmly observed, 'To have such a kind-hearted, affectionate sister must surely be a comfort to your brother.'

General Tilney saw and heard all of this in stern silence. He then opened a letter of his own. Having read its contents, he folded it and thrust it into his pocket. He banged his fist upon the table, stood up angrily, and marched out of the room. The others stared after him in frightened wonder.

After breakfast, Henry once again had to leave on parish business. He would be away for several days. As Eleanor had been called away by her father, Catherine was left alone to read over and over again her brother's letter. How had she so misread Isabella? She reflected that she had misread many things lately. Although stern, General Tilney was not a murderer; the cabinet did not contain secrets, and Isabella was a superficial and false friend. 'I have been such an idiot!' she exclaimed.

When the door softly opened and Eleanor, pale and trembling, stepped into the room, Catherine stared in surprise. 'My dear Catherine,' Eleanor's voice faltered and she stared at the ground. 'I am a most unwilling messenger ... my father says that you must leave Northanger Abbey within the next hour. Your carriage is already ordered.'

Catherine gasped. 'Have I offended the General?'

'I don't know why he is so angry. Oh Catherine, being the messenger, I seem guilty of the insult, but you know enough of my father to understand that I am powerless. You must at least allow me to help you to pack.'

And so it was, one hour later, that our heroine left Northanger Abbey in mystified sorrow and shame. General Tilney did not even offer the civility of a farewell. In a final, tearful embrace with Eleanor, Catherine whispered, 'Remember me to Henry.' Unable to say any more, she began the long journey home, alone. What had she done to anger the General? Had Henry told him her suspicions? What had been in his letter? What would Henry do when he heard?

Although she returned home from her adventures in shame rather than in glory, our heroine was greeted with joyful family love. Everybody marvelled at how she had changed during the three months she had been away. Over dinner, they shared her astonishment at the General's behaviour. 'He has been neither honourable nor sensitive,' observed Mrs

Morland. 'He must be a very strange man. Never mind,' she concluded wisely, 'we must all live and learn.'

In spite of the comfort of her family's love and common sense, Catherine's spirits remained low. For a week, she was unable to concentrate, unable to play with her younger siblings or do anything useful in the house.

A knock on the door one afternoon interrupted Mrs Morland's work. Catherine heard a visitor's voice below. 'My visit must be unwelcome after my father's rudeness, but I wonder whether I might be allowed to talk with your daughter.'

'Henry!' Catherine, anxious and agitated, managed enough composure to descend the stairs without falling. She accepted Henry's invitation to join him for a walk. As they walked, they talked. Henry assured Catherine of his affection and, in a flutter of happiness, she agreed to become his wife.

Secured of Catherine's heart, Henry then explained his father's behaviour.

Catherine's only crime had been that of being less wealthy than General Tilney had supposed. John and Isabella Thorpe had made incorrect assumptions about the wealth of the Morland family. That night at the theatre, Thorpe had boasted to the General about his own intention to marry Catherine, and about Isabella's friendship with James. Impressed by Thorpe's exaggerated reports of her family's wealth, General Tilney had decided to do all that he could to dash Thorpe's hopes and encourage the developing friendship between Catherine and Henry.

When Isabella and John Thorpe discovered the truth about the Morlands' wealth, Thorpe was furious. He wrote to General Tilney, informing him that his guest at Northanger Abbey was from a family of only moderate income. That letter had arrived the same morning as the letter from James, Catherine's explanation of which had confirmed Thorpe's comments. Furious, General Tilney had sent Catherine home.

'I am ashamed to report such things of my own father,' finished Henry, sadly. 'When I returned home and learnt how he had treated you, I argued with him as I have never before. I told him of my intention to come here immediately and ask you to marry me. I am afraid we do not yet have his blessing, but I believe that deep down, his main concern is his children's happiness. We must wait until he softens.'

Reader, I must now leave you to decide how long the happy couple had to wait until they were able to marry. I leave it to you to imagine the happiness of Eleanor and Catherine when they became sisters-in-law as well as friends. Finally, I leave it to you to decide how happily our hero and heroine lived ever after.

If Catherine and Henry do not conform to your usual expectations of a hero and heroine, I make no apology. Instead, all the credit of a wild and original imagination must be my own.

TAKING THINGS FURTHER

The real read

This *Real Read* version of *Northanger Abbey* is a retelling of Jane Austen's magnificent work. If you would like to read the full novel in all its original splendour, many complete editions are available, from bargain paperbacks to beautifully-bound hardbacks. You may well find a copy in your local charity shop.

Filling in the spaces

The loss of so many of Jane Austen's original words is a sad but necessary part of the shortening process. We have had to make some difficult decisions, omitting subplots and details, some important, some less so, but all interesting. We have also, at times, taken the liberty of combining two events into one, or of giving a character words or actions that originally belong to another. The points below will fill in some of the gaps, but nothing can beat the original.

- *Northanger Abbey* is Jane Austen's earliest major work. Her style is less refined in this than in her later works. We have tried to keep this difference in this *Real Reads* version.

- Catherine's father is a clergyman, which helps to explain why her family has only a moderate income, and why the Master of Ceremonies at the Pump Rooms feels it appropriate to introduce her to Henry Tilney.

- The progress of Catherine's friendships in Bath is slower than in this *Real Reads* version. She meets Henry before meeting the Thorpes, but does not meet Eleanor until a later occasion.

- Jane Austen writes amusingly of Catherine and Isabella's friendship, making Isabella's superficiality evident to the reader, but not to Catherine.

- Henry's words in defence of novels are actually the narrator's.

- When Isabella and Catherine are surprised to meet John and James, they are in the street, not at a ball.

- The main confusion about Catherine's wealth arises because the Thorpes expect her to inherit a considerable sum from Mr and Mrs Allen.

- John Thorpe engages Catherine for the first dance at a ball, but disappears into the card room. Catherine is then very disappointed when she has to turn down an invitation to dance with Henry in case John Thorpe reappears.

- On one occasion, Isabella encourages Catherine to lie to Eleanor, and John Thorpe actually gives a false excuse on Catherine's behalf. Catherine does what she believes to be right and remains honest.

- Catherine dines with the Tilneys before being invited to Northanger Abbey.

- Isabella develops a flirtatious relationship with Frederick Tilney, Henry's brother. It is for him that she abandons James. Catherine had tried to warn Henry about this, but he understood that Isabella was as much to blame as Frederick.

- Initially, General Tilney's treatment of Catherine makes it very clear that he wishes

Henry to marry her. They all visit Henry's home at Woodston.

● Knowing their father's interest in money, Henry and Eleanor are confused by his kindness towards Catherine, but say nothing about it. They do not share his belief in her wealth.

● General Tilney is not present when Catherine receives her letter from James, and he himself does not receive a letter. The General bumps into John Thorpe on a business visit to London. This is when Thorpe tells him the truth about Catherine's wealth.

● Isabella is soon abandoned by Frederick Tilney.

● The insult to Catherine in being sent away is immense. General Tilney does not even allow a servant to accompany her.

● General Tilney's attitude towards Catherine and Henry softens when Eleanor marries a wealthy man.

Back in time

Northanger Abbey is Jane Austen's earliest major novel, but was only published after her death.

Like Catherine, Jane Austen visited Bath as a young woman. Bath was then a highly fashionable place to visit: a place for amusement, romance and adventure for the upper classes. The Pump Rooms and the Upper and Lower Rooms were places of public assembly. The role of the Master of Ceremonies was to introduce well-suited people for friendship or romance.

In Jane Austen's time, the relationship between marriage and money was very important. Women were neither expected nor adequately educated to work for a living. Marrying a wealthy man was the most respectable way to gain independence and achieve comfort. Isabella is guided by this consideration when she ends her engagement to James Morland. John Thorpe, too, hopes to improve his social status by marriage. Henry and Catherine, however, will marry for love.

Reading books was one way for people to both better and entertain themselves. Gothic horror fictions became extremely popular in the 1790s. *The Mysteries of Udolpho* by Ann Radcliffe would have been well-known. Such works, considered 'light fiction', were bringing novels into disrepute, so much so that people might be tempted to deny that they enjoyed novels. Even Catherine, however, distinguishes between these and what she calls 'better books'. Jane Austen would probably have advocated extensive reading so that, like Henry Tilney, a reader could judge for themselves the value of different books.

Finding out more

We recommend the following books and websites to gain a greater understanding of Jane Austen's England:

Books

- Gill Hornby, *Who was Jane Austen? The Girl with the Magic Pen*, Short Books, 2005.

- Jon Spence, *Becoming Jane Austen*, Hambledon Continuum, 2007.

- Henrietta Webb and Josephine Ross, *Jane Austen's Guide to Good Manners: Compliments, Charades and Horrible Blunders*, Bloomsbury, 2006.

- Dominique Enwright, *The Wicked Wit of Jane Austen*, Michael O'Mara, 2007.

- Lauren Henderson, *Jane Austen's Guide to Romance: The Regency Rules*, Headline, 2007.

- Deirdre Le Faye, *Jane Austen: The World of Her Novels*, Frances Lincoln, 2003.

- Tom Tierney, *Fashions of the Regency Period Paper Dolls*, Dover, 2000.

Websites

- www.janeausten.co.uk
Home of the Jane Austen Centre in Bath, England.

- www.janeaustensoci.freeuk.com
Home of the Jane Austen Society. Includes summaries of, and brief commentaries on, her novels.

- www.pemberley.com

A very enthusiastic site for Jane Austen enthusiasts.

- www.literaryhistory.com/19thC/AUSTEN

A selective and helpful guide to links to other Jane Austen sites.

Film

- *Northanger Abbey* (1986), adapted and directed by Andrew Davies, BBC.

Food for thought

Here are some things to think about if you are reading *Northanger Abbey* alone, or ideas for discussion if you are reading it with friends.

In retelling *Northanger Abbey* we have tried to recreate, as accurately as possible, Jane Austen's original plot and characters. We have also tried to imitate aspects of her style. Remember, however, that this is not the original work; thinking about the points below, therefore, can help you begin to understand Jane Austen's craft.

To move forward from here, turn to the full-length version of *Northanger Abbey* and lose yourself in her wonderful portrayals of human nature.

Starting points

- Which character interests you the most? Why?

- How do you think Catherine's understanding develops during the course of her adventures?

- Consider the differences between Eleanor and Isabella.

- Consider the differences between John Thorpe and Henry Tilney.

- How do you think the first half of *Northanger Abbey* prepares readers for the events of the second half?

Themes

What do you think Jane Austen is saying about the following themes in *Northanger Abbey*?

- innocence and experience

- typical heroes and heroines
- friendship
- novels, and gothic novels in particular
- the relationship between wealth and marriage

Style

Can you find paragraphs containing examples of the following?

- a person exposing their true character through something they say
- humour
- gentle irony, where the writer makes the reader think one thing whilst saying something different; this is often a way of gently mocking one of the characters
- contrasts
- the narrator's voice

Look closely at how these paragraphs are written. What do you notice? Can you write a paragraph in the same style?